Cold Little
Duck, Duck, Duck

by Lisa Westberg Peters

Pictures by Sam Williams

MACMILLAN
CHILDREN'S BOOKS

First published in the United States in 2000 by Greenwillow Books,
an imprint of HarperCollins*Publishers*
First published in Great Britain in 2001 by Macmillan Children's Books
a division of Macmillan Publishers Limited
25 Eccleston Place, London SW1W 9NF
Basingstoke and Oxford
Associated companies throughout the world
www.macmillan.com

ISBN 0 333 96054 8 (HB)
ISBN 0 333 96055 6 (PB)

1 3 5 7 9 8 6 4 2

A CIP catalogue record for this book is available from the British Library.

Printed in Belgium

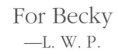

For Becky
—L. W. P.

For Linda—my spring in winter
—S. W.

One miserable
and frozen spring

bleak bleak bleak

A cold little
duck flew in

brisk
brisk brisk

Her pond was
stiff and white

creak creak creak

And her feet
froze to the ice

You're far
too early,
Duck, go

back

back

back

You're beginning
to shiver, Duck

shake

shake

shake

She tucked her
head into
her feathers to

wake

wake

wake

Her thoughts of spring and warmer weather

quick quick quick

Of bubbly streams

and glassy puddles

drink   drink   drink

Of wiggly worms and shiny beetles

black   black   black

Of crocuses and apple buds

pink

pink

pink

And blades of grass
in squishy mud

snack
snack
snack

Her thoughts
of spring
filled the sky

Until a V
of ducks
flew by

flock

flock

flock

They saw
that spring
was in the air

blink blink blink

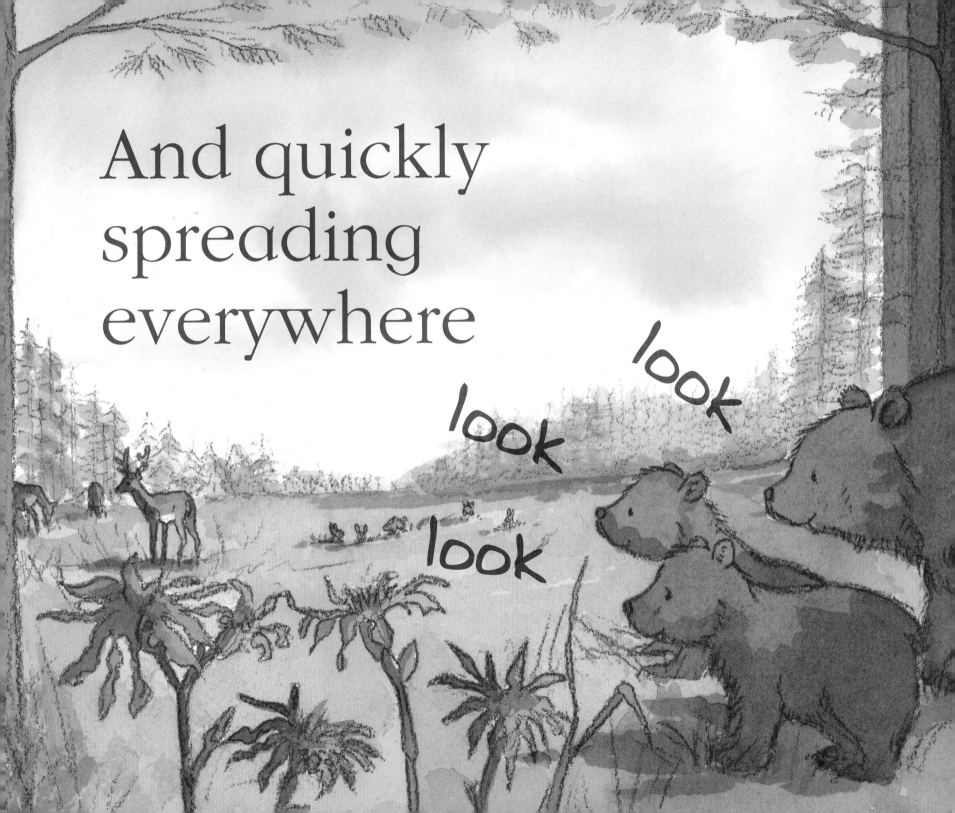

The ducks
flew down,
they dipped
and splashed

dunk dunk dunk

The cold little
duck began
to slide

slick slick slick

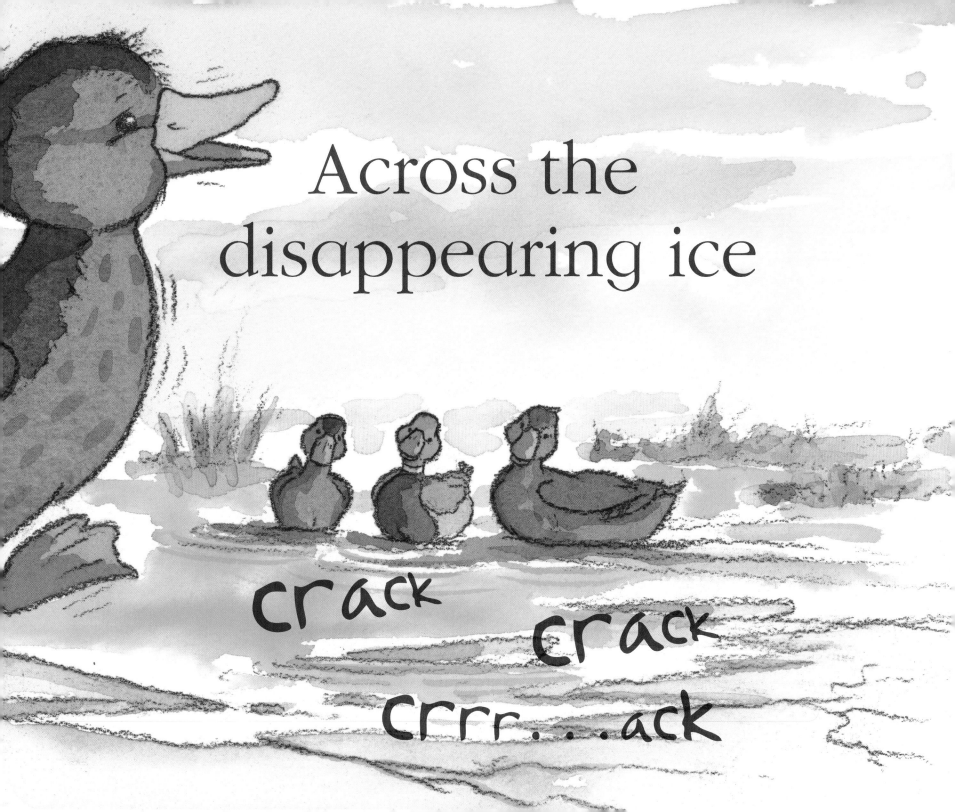

Across the
disappearing ice

crack

crack

crrr....ack

She wiggled
her tail,
waggled
her wings

kick

kick

kick

The warm little duck
dived into spring

quack quack